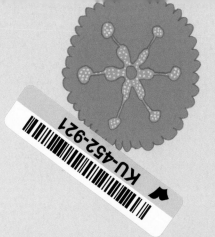

This Walker book
belongs to:

_____

_____

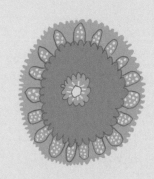

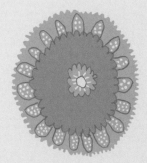

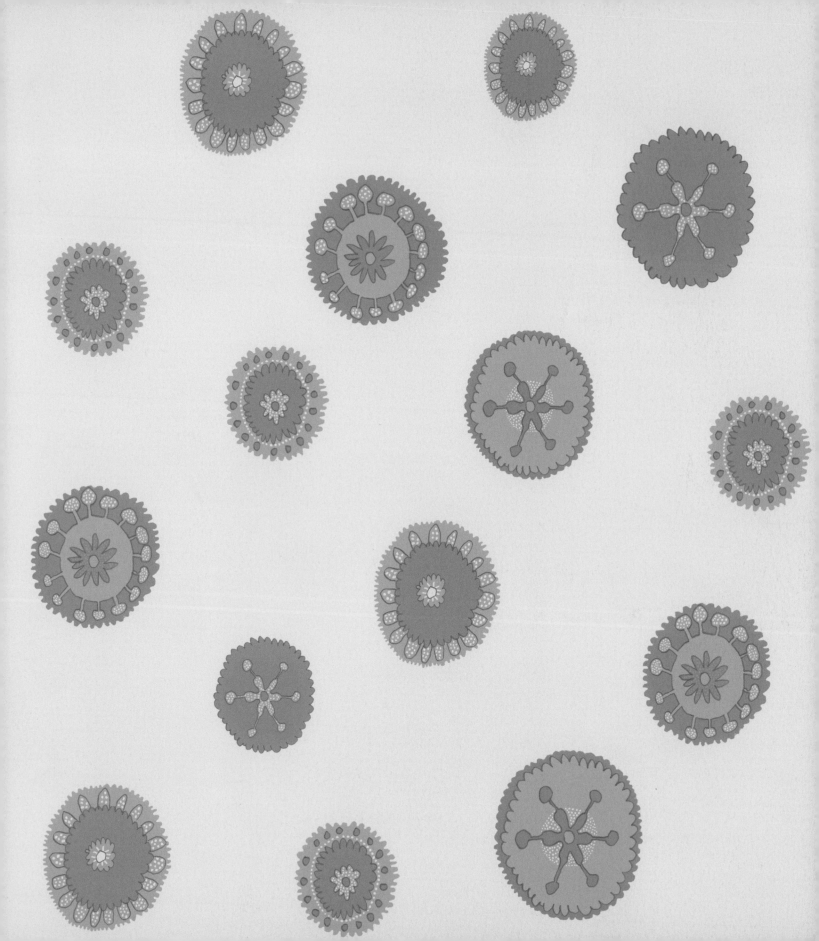

For Cooper Jacobson Reinfeld  F. M.

Welcome to the world, Angelo Graves  L. T.

First published in Great Britain 2015 by Walker Books Ltd
87 Vauxhall Walk, London SE11 5HJ

This edition published 2018

10 9 8 7 6 5 4 3 2 1

Text © 2015 Fran Manushkin
Illustrations © 2015 Lauren Tobia

The right of Fran Manushkin and Lauren Tobia
to be identified as the author and illustrator respectively
of this work has been asserted by them in accordance
with the Copyright, Designs and Patents Act 1988

This book has been typeset in Garamouche

Printed in China

British Library Cataloguing in Publication Data:
a catalogue record for this book is available
from the British Library

ISBN 978-1-4063-7888-7

www.walker.co.uk

# Happy in Our Skin

Fran Manushkin    illustrated by Lauren Tobia

WALKER BOOKS
AND SUBSIDIARIES
LONDON · BOSTON · SYDNEY · AUCKLAND

# Look at you!

You look so cute
in your brand-new birthday suit.
This is how we all begin:
small and happy in our skin.

Bouquets of babies
sweet to hold:
cocoa brown,
cinnamon,
and honey gold.

Ginger-coloured babies,
peaches and cream, too –
splendid skin for me,
splendid skin for you!

It's terrific to have skin.
It keeps the outsides out
and your insides in.

As you keep growing,
your skin grows, too.
Clever skin for me,
clever skin for you.

Whoops!
When you fall,
your skin will heal
with a scab,
a perfect seal.

Sometimes
skin has freckles
or birthmarks
or dimples.

We get a tan when it's sunny,
and when it's freezing –
goose pimples!

It's delightful
to hug
and tickle
and wrestle,

get a scratch when we itch,
and hold hands
and nestle.

Skin covers us from

head to toes.

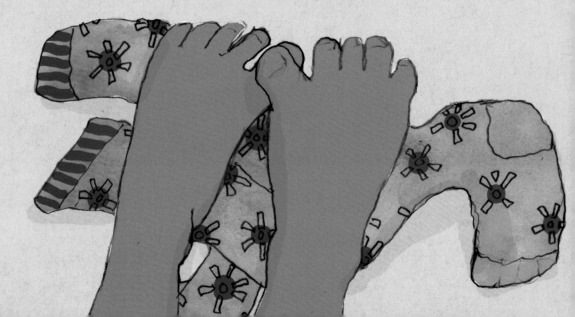

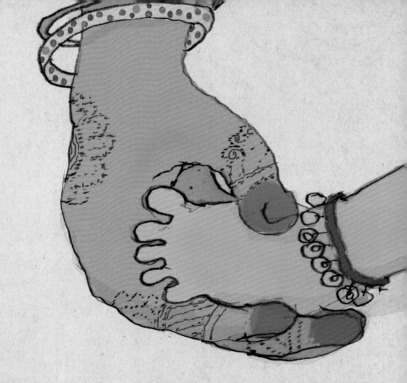

It's always there

beneath our clothes.

Yes, we all have skin,
but nobody is you.
You are one of a kind
and your fingerprints, too.

What a wonderful world!

Such a hullabaloo –

with all of us in it!

See the splendid view:

STREET PARTY

bouquets of people,
blooming and boisterous,
brawny and thin,
loving each day …

happy in our skin!

# Also illustrated by Lauren Tobia:

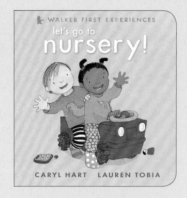

978-1-4063-6188-9

978-1-4063-6193-3

978-1-4063-7807-8

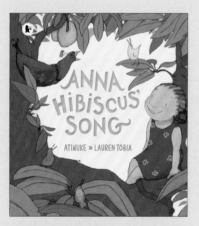

978-1-4063-3841-6

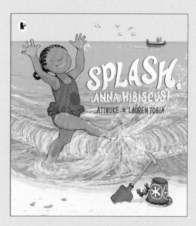

978-1-4063-5468-3

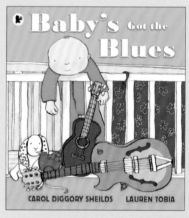

978-1-4063-6004-2

Fran Manushkin is the author of more than 50 books for children. She lives in New York City. Find her online at franmanushkin.com and on Twitter as @fmanushkin.

Lauren Tobia lives in Bristol with her husband and their two Jack Russell terriers, Poppy and Tilly. Find her online at laurentobia.com and on Twitter as @laurentobia.

**Available from all good booksellers**

www.walker.co.uk